KIDS CAN'T STOP READING
THE CHOOSE YOUR
OWN ADVENTURE® STORIES!

"Choose Your Own Adventure is the best thing that has come along since books themselves."
—Alysha Beyer, age 11

"I didn't read much before, but now I read my Choose Your Own Adventure books almost every night."
—Chris Brogan, age 13

"I love the control I have over what happens next."
—Kosta Efstathiou, age 17

"Choose Your Own Adventure books are so much fun to read and collect—I want them all!"
—Brendan Davin, age 11

And teachers like this series, too:
"We have read and reread, worn thin, loved, loaned, bought for others, and donated to school libraries our Choose Your Own Adventure books."

CHOOSE YOUR OWN ADVENTURE®—
AND MAKING READING MORE FUN!

Bantam Books in the Choose Your Own Adventure® Series
Ask your bookseller for the books you have missed.

THE BRILLIANT DR. WOGAN

BY R.A. MONTGOMERY

ILLUSTRATED BY LESLIE MORRILL

BANTAM BOOKS
TORONTO · NEW YORK · LONDON · SYDNEY · AUCKLAND

RL 4, IL age 10 and up

THE BRILLIANT DR. WOGAN
A Bantam Book / August 1987

CHOOSE YOUR OWN ADVENTURE® *is a registered trademark of Bantam Books Inc. Registered in U.S. Patent and Trademark Office and elsewhere.*
Original conception of Edward Packard.

ISBN 0-553-26724-8

Published simultaneously in the United States and Canada

Bantam Books are published by Bantam Books, Inc. Its trademark, consisting of the words "Bantam Books" and the portrayal of a rooster, is registered in U.S. Patent and Trademark Office and in other countries. Marca Registrada. Bantam Books, Inc., 666 Fifth Avenue New York, New York 10103.

PRINTED IN THE UNITED STATES OF AMERICA

O   0 9 8 7 6 5 4 3 2 1

THE BRILLIANT
DR. WOGAN

WARNING!!!

Do not read this book straight through from beginning to end! These pages contain many different adventures you may have as you search for the brilliant Dr. Wogan. From time to time as you read along, you will be able to make choices. Your choice may lead to success or disaster.

The adventures you have will be the results of those choices. After you make your choice, follow the instructions to see what happens to you next.

Remember—you are not the only one looking for the missing genius. The device in his possession is sought by the whole world. . . . Will you be the first one to find him?

"There isn't a clue. Not a trace! Wogan, the brilliant Doctor Wogan, is gone."

The fat, stoop-shouldered official in the rumpled gray suit slams his pencil on the desk and sits down, not looking at anyone in the room. You glance around at the others. They are all silent.

Then, without warning, you hear:

"There is only one person who can find Wogan and bring him back—if he's alive. We all know who I'm talking about. *You,* come up here." The man in the gray suit points at you.

You are the youngest scientist ever to be a member of the world-famous Delta Group, a research team made up of people from both the small and the powerful countries, dedicated to global peace. Wogan is the head of the group, and you are his right-hand assistant.

Turn to page 2.

2

The year is 2012, and the world has been at the edge of nuclear war for more than sixty years. Wogan has concentrated his research on a device that neutralizes radiation. "Just think," he has often said to you, "we can make nuclear weapons powerless if this device works."

"But Doctor Wogan," you replied recently, "in the wrong hands the radiation neutralizer could hold the world hostage. One group or country would be safe from attack, but the rest of the world wouldn't be."

"I know," he said. "That is why I must hurry to finish the device and give it to the entire world—so that everyone can have it."

Turn to page 9.

You have no opportunity to surrender. The next rocket explodes in the villa, ending all opportunity for action, now or in the future.

The End

4

The ferry for Bozcaada is an old boat, grimy with years of service. Barnacles and seaweed cling to its hull. It sloshes up and down in the gentle swell of the Aegean.

"One ticket," you say to the man selling tickets.

"One way or return?" he asks in surprisingly good English.

"Return, I hope," you reply.

"As you wish," he murmurs, handing you your ticket.

The ferry does not depart for two hours. When at last it chugs away from Canakkale, you survey the other passengers—there are six of them.

Turn to page 19.

6

The square is filled with people. The man who bumped into you is nowhere to be seen. He has been absorbed into the crowd of busy people on market day.

"Well, here I go," you say. "The island can wait until another day."

"What's that?" an old woman asks, staring up at you out of a wrinkled face with milky blue eyes.

"Nothing! Nothing! Just talking to myself," you reply.

The woman stares at you for a few more moments, then she too is gone, swallowed up by the crowd of market-goers. The sun is fading in the late afternoon sky, and the air is growing cool. You pull your jacket tight, zip it up, and look for the Hotel Christos.

Turn to page 10.

The action inhibitor is a typical Wogan creation. It freezes people in time, rendering them harmless without hurting them.

You were chosen by Wogan two years ago to be his right-hand assistant. Brains, imagination, courage, and will to succeed were the qualities that made Wogan select you. Those were heady days for you. Wogan, a true genius, believed in developing people's real talents and gifts.

"People use only a fraction of their ability. We must unlock true human potential," he was fond of saying.

And you succeeded. Brilliantly. Then Wogan, his work at its height, disappeared. Was it his choice or was he kidnapped?

You guess that it was his intention to escape before he was kidnapped along with the plans for the nearly completed radiation neutralizer. But did he succeed? There have been rumors and fears that agents for both private groups and governments want that device, since with it they could terrorize the world, remaining untouched themselves, in the event of retaliatory strikes.

Turn to page 36.

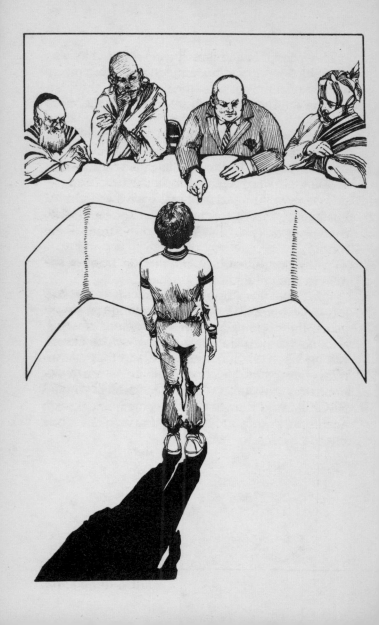

The next day Wogan disappeared. He was probably kidnapped by someone or some group who wanted the plans for the device. But there is a chance that he has gone into hiding to work in safety.

Now you sit in Delta Group Conference Room B in a research complex just south of London. You don't protest when the official calls you forward. They would never take no for an answer, and besides, as Wogan's assistant you probably are most qualified to search for the genius. You rise slowly from your chair and walk toward the front of the room.

You place yourself at attention in front of the man in the gray suit.

"So," he says, "you know how important this job is. Without Wogan the work of the last eleven years, the hope of hundreds of millions of souls, and maybe even life as we know it on this planet, will be lost. L-O-S-T forever. It's sad that we humans have gotten to a point where so much depends on one person, but we have. BRING HIM BACK ALIVE! Remember, there are many foreign agents after him and his plans. You won't be alone in your search for Wogan."

Turn to page 88.

The Hotel Christos is across from the church. It is in an old stone building with thick oak doors.

You take a deep breath and enter the hotel. It is dark and gloomy inside. You have a feeling this isn't an ordinary hotel.

A dwarf dressed in a fancy scarlet uniform greets you with an unusually loud voice. "May I be of service?"

"Yes," you reply. "I want to sign up for Zabillh's show."

"Oh! So you want to see the Great Zabillh perform? I might have known. Well, follow me. I will take you to sign up. Be careful, the ceiling is low and the steps are uneven." He leads you toward the back of the dark lobby.

Turn to page 82.

You wish you could hide somewhere, but you are bathed in the harsh cabin light. Any sudden movement would be noticed. The Yenrotta moves slowly toward your table. He is staring right at you. His eyes have taken on a new look, an intense, burning gaze of recognition. At that moment you catch sight of the woman. She moves from behind a group of people, holding a weapon in her hand. The Yenrotta does not seem to see her. The next thing you know, the woman is surrounded by a group of passengers and disarmed. Shuddering, you await your fate. The Yenrotta speaks. "You are a troublesome and difficult person. But we do have a place for your kind, don't we?" The Yenrotta looks at the passengers. They nod. You realize the passengers aren't tourists. They're all working together.

"So off we go to a nice room at the Hotel Christos. You will be comfortable there and we'll be able to keep an eye on you. You won't interfere with our plans, and we'll have a chance to get to know one another. We have a lot to talk about. Wogan and the radiation neutralizer, for example." He smiles a very unpleasant smile. You smile back. You might as well be pleasant. You have a feeling you and the Yenrotta will be spending a lot of time together.

The End

12

Wogan once told you that sound currents connected all things in the universe. Some sounds could be used for good; other sounds created evil. Now that you think back to those days in Wogan's labs and testing grounds, you recall the presence of soothing sound.

"Lead on," you hear yourself say in a distant voice, almost as if you are hearing a recording of your voice played in a tunnel.

You feel yourself drifting. You are relaxed, able to see clearly but unable to think quickly or normally. You are led away.

"I'm hypnotized," you say out loud. But your voice is a mere whisper.

Turn to page 97.

"Help!" you shout, desperately working the switch.

Suddenly the switch slides to the "on" position. The magnetic field reverser goes into immediate effect. There is a massive shuddering sound and a vibration so unsettling that you frantically try to return the switch to "off." You don't succeed.

Turn to page 101.

14

"You can't scare me. Wogan is too powerful for you. You're bluffing. I'm leaving, and if you try to prevent me or harm me, you will pay. Look at this, and look at it carefully." You remove the energy minimizer from your pocket and display it.

The small black object in your hand looks harmless, but the four people stare at it as if it were alive and could bite.

"I'm leaving now. I'm not kidding. Follow me, and it's your funeral."

You mount the first rung of the stairs with your back turned to the three. You hear a sound. You stop. Slowly you turn. You finger the energy minimizer. No one moves.

If you decide to switch on the energy minimizer, turn to page 27.

If you run up the spiral stairs, turn to page 41.

16

Carefully you examine the room, checking the walls, the floor, the bank of computer screens. The screens are blank, giving off only the greenish light.

You turn away from them, frustrated. And in your frustration, you become careless.

By accident, *you switch the action inhibitor off!* Within seconds you are in handcuffs and old-fashioned leg irons. The dwarf, carrying a flashlight, leads you to a windowless cell. You are infuriated by your own foolishness. You note with dismay a high watermark indicating flooding near the ceiling. You may be doomed. Only time will tell.

The cell door clamps shut.

The End

A stout middle-aged man steps into the room.

"Come now, my good friend, you've had a bad time of it. Let's leave these dreary surroundings and see if we can have a pleasant little talk. Follow me."

Moments later you emerge from the subterranean chamber via a tunnel into a bright garden. The sun is at its zenith. You wonder how much time has passed. The digital read-out on your watch tells you it's noon.

"Wogan is with us," the man says. "However, he is, how should I say it? He is sick, or rather, incapacitated, at the moment. Perhaps you could help him."

"How?" you ask suspiciously.

"Well, interpret these papers of his, and we'll release him to you. Simple. No risk," the man says. He hands you a sheaf of papers. You recognize at once what they are. They are Wogan's plans for the unfinished radiation neutralizer. They are, however, missing important bits of information.

"How did you get these?" you ask.

"We have our ways," he replies.

Turn to page 108.

The six passengers spread throughout the small cabin, each taking a seat near one of the windows. You have been traveling for several hours when one of them, a young woman dressed in a yellow rain slicker, motions to you with a nod of her head and a slight movement of her hand. She repeats the movement and looks aft at the deck at the stern of the cabin. Then she gets up and leaves the cabin.

You are about to rise and follow her when a man, middle-aged and well-dressed in a suit and a tweed overcoat, attracts your attention by dropping a cigarette lighter. He bends to pick it up, and while rising, gently shakes his head, looks at the figure of the woman who is now out on deck and mouths the word, "No."

If you decide to ignore the man's warning and go out on deck to talk to the woman, go on to the next page.

If you decide to take the man's advice and not follow the woman, turn to page 92.

Rising slowly to accommodate the swell of the waves, you ignore the frowning man and move outside the cabin. A moist and salty sea breeze greets you. It has already grown dark. The woman standing next to the rail doesn't look at you. You take a position next to her. Both of you stare into the plume of white foam streaming behind the ferry.

Finally she speaks.

"You are in great danger. I am your only friend on this boat. Beware of the others. Stay close to me and speak to no one. Wogan awaits." She still doesn't look at you. You have no opportunity to read what is in her eyes: truth or lies.

"Who are the others?" you ask.

"Your enemies! Yours and Wogan's and the world's. I can't say more. It is not important anyway."

You remember the note. It said you'd be contacted, but it did not say where or when. Is this woman your contact? Is the man who dropped the lighter your contact?

Go on to the next page.

Out of the corner of your eye you become aware of movement inside the cabin. Two men are tiptoeing toward the door leading to the aft deck. You start to warn the woman that the men are coming, but suddenly you notice the glint of light on a metal object in the woman's hand.

If you jump ship and swim for the island, turn to page 63.

If you warn the woman that the men are coming, turn to page 22.

"They're coming for us," you whisper loudly.

"Let them come," she replies. The cold tone of her voice frightens you.

The two men have reached the deck. They split up, one taking the port side and the other the starboard side, slowly moving in on the two of you.

"Okay, don't you move or you'll force me to do something we'll all regret," says the smaller of the two men. He holds a blunt-nosed revolver. The other man fingers a gleaming stiletto.

You back up, praying for a miracle. The woman laughs and points the shiny metal object at them.

Turn to page 35.

Swimming in the wake of the ferry is difficult, but you do your best. The water is very cold.

You've swum several yards when you see a rowboat bob over a wave. A man smoking a pipe leans over the side.

"Get in before you freeze to death," he says in a heavily accented voice.

Grasping the gunwale, you climb aboard the small rowboat. You shiver fiercely.

"Here, drink this and put this coat on," he says.

The man hands you a cup of steaming hot soup from a thermos and gives you a wrinkled gray-green army overcoat.

The ferry has turned around. Its searchlights are scanning the water. Two rockets have gone up in arcs. Their light illuminates a large stretch of water, but the rowboat is outside the circle of light, at least for now.

"Here, shoot out the searchlights," the man says, handing you a rifle with a long-range night scope attached to its slender barrel. He is busy fitting an outboard motor to the stern of the rowboat.

"I didn't count on rockets, but they will burn out. Shoot out the searchlights. Those people mean to kill you."

Go on to the next page.

Why is this man so conveniently there in a boat? Is he friend or enemy? Who are your friends? Wogan's friends? As you wonder about these things, a motor launch carrying three people starts out from the ferry. It's headed in your direction.

If you agree to follow the man's command, turn to page 46.

If you decide to ignore him, turn to page 38.

The story then tells of a dangerous period when the leader escapes to a remote island. As you read on, you begin to realize that the story is actually what has just been happening. It ends successfully because of the return and help of a trusted young associate. You gasp in amazement. There on the page is your own name! The date of the story is today! You drop the book, suddenly frightened. Somehow you have gotten your hands on a book from the future. You wonder if Wogan had a hand in this. You are then flooded with a wonderful sense of well-being. You place the book on the floor and sit cross-legged in a meditation pose Wogan once showed you.

The van bumps along the road leading to your destiny. Whatever happens is clearly beyond your control.

The End

"I warned you," you shout, pointing the energy minimizer directly at the group. "Here goes."

The click of the "on" button reverberates in the room. You wait. At first nothing seems to happen. Then one of the people slowly raises an arm, drawing a pistol from a narrow black belt cinched around his waist. You realize the movements are all in slow motion.

It takes minutes for the person to raise the object, aim it, and fire.

"Zeeck . . ."

Turn to page 59.

Lunging forward, you stumble on the next step. Somewhere below you one of the people pulls out a weapon and fires. The first blast is wide of its mark. A bullet pulverizes a block of stone and ricochets off the metal handrail of the spiral staircase just below you.

"How did I ever get into this?" you ask yourself as you desperately climb the remaining steps.

Their weapon needs reloading, giving you precious time, but two of the attackers are close behind you on the stairs.

Turn to page 96.

You recall Wogan's often-repeated words: "Escape is central to all planning. You must always have an alternate route." Before taking one more step, you need to evaluate your options. The one thing the dwarf forgot to do was search you. Had he done so, he would have discovered three devices, all small, all electronic, all harmless-looking, but powerful tools, nevertheless.

One of the devices is an action inhibitor, designed by Wogan to make an aggressor incapable of taking action—without harming him. Another device is an energy minimizer, a radical new device intended to slow down all molecular activity. Bullets float, punches seem cushioned in sponge, sound falls to pieces as if decaying. This device has never been used. The long-term effects are unknown. It is a spin-off from the radiation neutralizer.

The third device is something called a magnetic field reverser. It can be dangerous to the user.

You slip your hand into your jacket pocket, trying to decide on the proper device and the best strategy. Should you use the action inhibitor or the energy minimizer? Either way you have the magnetic field reverser as a backup.

If you decide to use the action inhibitor, turn to page 7.

If you favor the energy minimizer, turn to page 14.

"Wogan is my only . . ." you say, your voice trailing off until it's inaudible. You slump against the wall and slip to the floor with a bone-jarring thud. Your eyes roll, you drool, and you speak garbled words. It is only half play-acting, since you hit your head hard when you fell. At least the sudden movement released you from the hypnotic trance.

Turn to page 48.

Once safely on the dock, you survey the crowd, looking for a contact.

"Special bus to the castle. Great views, tourist special. Here's your ticket," says a man holding out a piece of paper. You look at the paper and see the name "Wogan" spelled out in big letters. The man nods and smiles. He gets in the bus and you follow.

The woman from the boat is already there! She's sitting next to a window. She motions to you to sit next to her. "Why didn't you come out on deck? I wanted to warn you about the opposition."

"I was scared, I guess. I didn't know who you were. I still don't."

"I'm Wogan's daughter," she replies. "And we are in danger, in even greater danger than I first thought. The opposition thinks you are Wogan's special courier. They will do anything to track you. It is a critical time. I give you a dangerous choice. Wogan has asked to see you, but if you will leave the bus, sacrificing yourself by serving as a decoy, Wogan may escape, taking with him the possibility of a peaceful world. We have already rescued him from crooks and spies in Canakkale, thanks to you. The crooks were distracted by your arrival and Wogan was able to break away from them as they tried to follow you."

Go on to the next page.

"And if I refuse to be a decoy?" you ask.

"Then stay aboard the bus and we will do our best to lose them and help Wogan escape."

If you decide to be a decoy, turn to page 39.

If you stay on the bus and go see Wogan, turn to page 51.

"I'll give them just enough information to tantalize them," you decide.

"What do you want to know?" you ask.

The voice comes from one corner of the room. "We have Wogan, but he went into a trance. He will not communicate with us. We fear he will die, and we are helpless to prevent this. If he dies, it will be a tragic loss to the world; we can't let it happen. We know you are close to Wogan and that you know about the radiation neutralizer. Help us."

"Well, what do you want?"

"Make him come out of the trance. We are a friendly private peace group. We only want to help. He thinks we're thieves. He said he'd die before dealing with us." The voice pauses. Then it continues.

"What proof does he need of our good intentions? We only wish to protect him from the *real* thieves. We got to him just to protect him—him and the world. There are greedy people out there who will do *anything* to get their hands on the only complete plans for the radiation neutralizer. If you know the final phases of the design, your life will be in danger. You'll be finished. But if you help us publicize the plans, then all the world will have the neutralizer. That's the only way to insure peace."

Turn to page 47.

A fine mist shoots out and envelops the two men. They are immediately turned into laughing, giggling, friendly people. The short one flings his revolver over the side of the ferry as though it were an unwanted and loathesome thing. The man with the knife drops it into the water.

"Now you will both sit down on the deck and wait until dawn. Is that understood?" the woman says to the two of them.

"Yes. Sure. Why not?" they answer, almost in unison.

"What now?" you ask her.

"We wait until we dock. Then you either return to the mainland because—wisely—you fear for your life, or you throw in with us. We can't spend time with the faint-hearted. This is serious business, and personal safety and survival are of little importance. Wogan has spoken highly of you. And thanks to you, he has just managed to escape a band of thieves in Canakkale. They were distracted by your arrival and wanted to follow you."

Soon the ferry docks, and the landing ramp bumps into place. The two men are still under the effect of the gas. The woman looks at you, waiting for your decision.

If you decide to stay aboard the ferry and return to the mainland to work out a plan or to get help, turn to page 42.

If you decide to land and go to Wogan, turn to page 103.

36

"Back to reality," you remind yourself. The action inhibitor in your hand gives you a feeling of power. Its effects should buy you time to investigate this suspicious group. All you have to do is push the switch.

You push it.

"ZAM!"

Time freezes. The dwarf and the others are stop-action frozen. Their mouths are open as if speaking, arms and legs stuck in ridiculous poses, eyes open, unblinking and unseeing. Only you are free from this effect.

You have seen it work in the lab. Wogan said no harm would come to anyone under the power of the inhibitor.

You walk over to the man who seemed to be in charge and wave your hand in front of his face. No response. You speak to him.

"Not too scary now, are you?" you say.

No response.

"I guess it really works. What now?" you ask yourself.

*If you decide to search for Wogan,
turn to page 16.*

If you decide to escape, turn to page 93.

The rifle rests on the seat next to you. You make no attempt to use it, despite his commands.

Once again you are in a situation beyond your control, a prisoner of circumstances, events, and *maybe* of this pipe-smoking man who has pulled you out of the sea.

"What are you doing out here?" you ask him.

"Some say I was fishing," he answers, busying himself with an outboard motor.

"Fishing for what? At night, without running lights on your boat? Sounds odd to me," you reply.

"Well, look what I caught," he replies, smiling at you.

You don't like the gleam in his eyes.

Turn to page 55.

"I'll go," you say, summoning up all your courage. "If it gives Wogan time to escape, it's what I must do."

The woman nods, and you get up from your seat. Your legs feel like they're weighted with lead, your feet seem to be unattached to your legs, and time seems dizzying and unreal. You move in a dreamlike state down the bus aisle, down two steps, and down the street outside, all the while waiting for a hail of bullets or worse.

Nothing happens. The bus starts up and moves off in a puff of diesel exhaust. You head for a taxi stand by a café across the small town square. People are milling about in the night, a mixture of tourists and locals. You try to look unconcerned, but your heart is beating so loudly that you fear the people on the street can hear it.

Turn to page 53.

The four people stay still. They must know about Wogan's inventions.

You mount the stairs, hoping their fear of your weapon will buy you some time. There's a movement behind you. You start to run. They are after you!

"Stop!" someone shouts. "Stop!"

You spin around and aim the energy minimizer at them, but to your horror it slips from your grasp and clatters down the spiral staircase, thudding to a stop on the stone floor of the chamber.

"Give up," they yell, almost in unison.

You look up toward the top of the stairs, feeling for the other two devices in your pocket.

"Rely on instinct," you tell yourself. "That's what Wogan would do in a case like this."

If you run for it, turn to page 28.

If you use one of the other devices, turn to page 57.

The woman sounds like a fanatic, you think, and a fanatic is useless in helping Wogan.

For a few more moments you survey the scene: two giggling men sitting on the deck, a dedicated woman waiting for your answer, and a crowd of people leaving the ferry. A man on the dock attracts your attention. Tall, stocky, bearded and deadly serious, he is closely watching every person who leaves.

"He's looking for me. I know it. I can feel it in my bones," you say.

"Who? Where?" the woman asks quickly.

"Over there. That man," you reply.

"It's a Yenrotta!" the woman exclaims, turning her head and ducking behind you.

"A what?" you ask.

"A Yenrotta. A gun for hire. Don't ask questions. Just move into the main cabin and wait. Let's hope he didn't see us."

Turn to page 67.

You reach for the device, but the delay has given your pursuers ample opportunity to catch up with you and surround you.

Your arms are pulled back, and handcuffs are snapped in place.

"Come with us. Be calm and we will not harm you. We want your help, not your life. You are so fearful. All peole seem to be that way, even the great Doctor Wogan. Pity. If only you didn't fear the unknown so much. Oh, well. In time, perhaps." The voice is calm and soothing. You relax and allow yourself to be led away.

Turn to page 84.

44

You move toward the door. Odd, you think to yourself, that you had not noticed the dull green metal door. Perhaps you were too frightened to be aware of your surroundings.

Three steps, four, then two more and you reach out and push. The door yields. Soon you will make your getaway.

But when you enter the brightly lit room, you find that you are not alone. Before you are two figures. They stand with arms folded, feet wide apart, forming a barrier to someone behind them—Wogan. They look grim and dangerous.

At that precise moment Wogan gathers all his energy, all his great willpower, and creates a miniature explosion that terminates all beings in a radius of twelve feet. You, of course, are included.

The End

"Okay, but I'm not very good with weapons—never had much desire to use them," you say.

The man pauses for a moment, giving the engine-mounting brackets one last twist. He pushes the outboard down so that the small propeller is in the sea. Before pulling the starter cord he says quietly, "Aim high. Squeeze the trigger—don't pull it. Fire again if you don't succeed."

"But there are people aboard the ferry! What if I hit them?" you cry, scared and worried.

"Too bad for them! There are victims everywhere in the world. That is just bad luck. Now, fire!"

You shake your head and put the gun down on the seat next to you. "No, I can't do it. I don't want to kill anyone. It's wrong," you say.

"Suit yourself. It's your life. I'll do it."

He grabs the rifle, aims, and squeezes the trigger. There is a popping sound, a small flash, and then the main searchlight on the ferry winks out. The man fires again. The ferry's other light goes out. Now only the bright white flares remain, and they are about to fall into the sea.

The motor launch from the ferry is heading for you.

Turn to page 68.

You don't believe the man. "This is no peace group," you say to yourself. "They're crooks."

Wogan once told you that in the event of serious trouble, you were to do your best to return to his private laboratory and either destroy the plans or have the completed ones published yourself. His greatest fear was that the plans would fall into the wrong hands.

"Why not publish them now?" you had asked.

"They're not finished," he had replied sadly.

At the very least, you were never to give any help to Wogan if he were a prisoner. He preferred death to giving up the plans.

If you decide to try to get Wogan out of his trance and save his life anyway, turn to page 74.

If you decide to try to escape, turn to page 52.

48

The room spins, the light intensifies, your head begins to clear, but you pretend to remain only semi-conscious. Slowly you open your eyes, millimeter by millimeter, surveying the room through your eyelashes.

It's empty! You sit up.

"They're gone," you sigh in relief. You feel your legs and arms, your head, your hands. Everything seems all right. You stagger to your feet and begin an investigation of the surrounding area.

A door in the stone wall attracts your attention. To your surprise, it opens.

Turn to page 17.

"I'm going with you, Wogan," you say.

"Okay. Our escape will be dangerous and exhausting. I'll be glad to have you along, my dear friend."

You nod your agreement.

Preparations are made in quiet.

Finally, you and Wogan are in a boat. You cast off and bid farewell to your silent companions on shore: several men and the bus driver. They will act as decoys for the enemy. Wogan's daughter has already left for a safe house inland. An hour later, as you sail quietly through the heaving sea, you see a brilliant flash of light. You think that it is probably an explosion at the villa. You are concerned about those left behind, but what you must concentrate on is what's ahead.

At dawn you reach land. You abandon the boat and head inland.

Turn to page 66.

"Hey, I'm no sitting duck for anyone!" you exclaim. "I'm here to help, but *that's* crazy. It sounds like suicide. Besides, you said Wogan wanted to see me."

"As you wish," she replies.

The bus moves off, and minutes later it is traveling along a narrow bumpy road, perilously close to a cliff that falls straight to the ocean below. The bus driver has turned out the lights and is driving very fast. You hope he knows what he's doing.

Turn to page 56.

52

"This won't be easy," you say to the man. "Wogan is strong, perhaps the strongest-willed person I have ever met. If he doesn't want to give information to you, nothing will get him out of the trance. But I will try. Perhaps he has misjudged you and your intentions."

The man nods his head vigorously in agreement with your notion that Wogan may have misunderstood. "Yes, yes. Very good. We intend no harm," he says earnestly. "We are anxious for the world to receive Wogan's great plans. That is all. We are for *peace* only. Wogan is in that room," he says, pointing. "Behind that green door."

"I must be alone with him," you say. The man nods agreement, stands back, and lets you pass.

You don't like the looks of that man. He probably spells *peace* G-R-E-E-D, you think.

Turn to page 44.

"Taxi!" you say in what you hope is a normal tone.

A cab pulls up. Its driver leans out the window.

"Yes, my friend," he says, "and where do you wish to go?"

You think for a moment. "Around the island. Yes, that's it, around the island. Just a little night-time tour," you reply.

"But of course, my pleasure."

Turn to page 76.

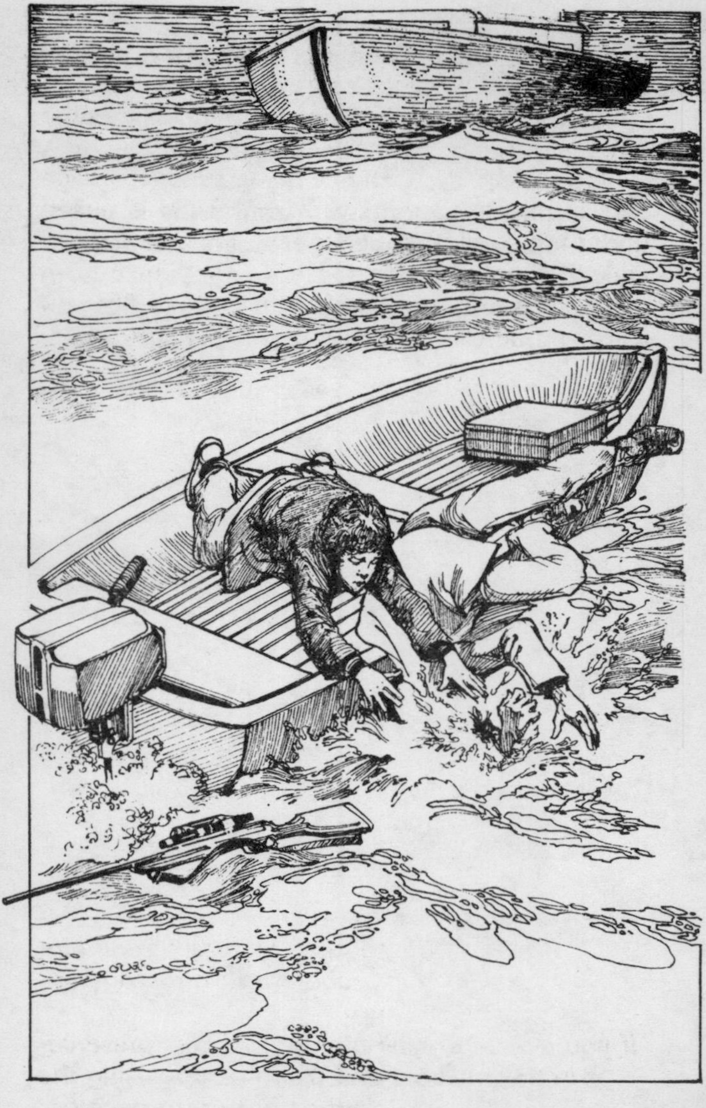

The man leans over, picks up the rifle, aims at the ferry boat, and just as he is about to fire, you lunge at him, knocking him and the gun into the sea.

"Hey! Help, I . . ." he yells in a splutter of rage and surprise. "I can't swim!" His head is pulled under the swell, then reappears. He tries desperately to cling to the boat. The motor launch from the ferry is nearing. The fear in his eyes fills you with sympathy. You know you can't let him drown.

If you decide to take the time to pull him aboard, turn to page 65.

If you decide to give him the only life preserver in the rowboat and try to escape using the outboard, turn to page 61.

Thirty minutes later the bus slides to a stop in the gravel courtyard of a gray stone villa perched at the edge of the sea. You see several figures move from the shadows of a high wall. They approach the bus cautiously.

"Is the person here?" one asks carefully.

"Yes," the driver replies.

You realize that they are talking about you.

"Wogan wants to leave immediately. I think it is dangerous just now. He will be exposed if he leaves. We can protect him here," says one of the men.

"Well, you know Wogan. He does what he wants," the driver says. "How about this one? What does Wogan want this person for?" They are speaking about you again.

"Wogan says this is the one who can help him with the plans," the first man replies.

Turn to page 70.

You grab one of the devices, not bothering to check which one it is. The on-off button sticks! It won't move!

If you decide to try the last remaining device, turn to page 43.

If you force the on—off switch, turn to page 13.

"We can't stay here and be targets," you shout from the floor. "Is there a hidden way out?"

"Quick. The basement stairs lead to a tunnel exit in the water," says one of the men. "Follow me."

Moments later you all stand knee-deep in water, wrestling with an old fishing boat, trying desperately to free it from its mooring. Behind you, a second shell explodes.

"I thought we were going to fight," you say.

"Against those weapons?" comes the answer.

Finally the boat is freed. The others climb in.

"Coming?" they ask you.

"No. I'll stay and see if I can buy you and Wogan more time."

They leave, only to be intercepted by a launch a mile offshore.

You stay, waiting for the worst.

The End

The bullet burbles through the air, tumbling and wavering. It falls to the ground and bounces like rubber. Then it melts into a million shimmering pieces, like bits of confetti, that spill over the stone floor.

"Try again," you say, taunting the group. *"Zleep!"*

Once again, a bullet is emitted from the muzzle of the weapon. This time it decays in mid-flight and drops harmlessly to the floor!

You stare at the object in your hand and begin to laugh. "Good old Wogan," you say. "He's done it again!"

At that moment the four people make a dash for you. The effects of the energy minimizer must be wearing off!

Turn to page 98.

60

"This might be my last chance," you say to yourself, struggling as hard as you can against your captors. You kick, butt with your head and swing your hands and arms in a wide arc, hoping to strike anyone in range.

"Calm down! No one is going to hurt you," commands a firm and familiar voice. "We had to make it look realistic, grabbing you the way we did, but we're not your enemy."

"Tell me another," you reply.

One of the men steps forward and strips off a plastic mask.

"Wogan!" you shout, amazed and happy at finding your friend.

"Correct. Now let's get out of here. By the way, this is my daughter," he says, motioning to the woman from the boat.

The End

"Take this. Good luck," you say, tossing the yellow canvas life jacket to the man floundering in the water.

"I'll drown," he wails, kicking and spluttering.

"Use the life jacket. Stay calm. Wait for your friends," you tell him.

"They're not my friends!" he screams.

The motor starts; you push him off the side of the boat, making sure he is in the life jacket, and head toward the darkened shoreline of the island.

Turn to page 104.

SPLASH!

The shock of the cold water almost knocks you out. You jumped far enough out to escape the terrible suction of the ferry's propellers, but now you are fighting to regain the surface in a froth of bubbles. The wake pummels you. At long last you reach the surface, gasping for breath.

"Where is it?" you say out loud, getting a mouthful of salt water for your effort. "Where is Bozcaada?"

The ferry plows on, and you see three people on the stern. You can't tell whether they are pointing at you, struggling with the woman, or trying to help you. A second later there's a splash off the stern.

"It's probably a life preserver," you say to yourself. "I hope it's not one of them, dead or alive."

Turn to page 24.

The van is moving on a bumpy road. You wait until things have been quiet for a while. Then, summoning all your strength and energy, you kick out of the burlap bag with an enormous lurching thrust. Your hands fly up, ready to strike anyone. "YIIOW!" you shout.

There is no one with you in the back of the van. You are alone! The van looks completely empty. Then you notice something peculiar: on the floor of the van lies a book. A bookmark of red leather is stuck in it. There is no title on the cover or the spine. As you are examining the book, the rear door swings open as the van hits a bump.

If you want to open the book, turn to page 80.

If you forget the book and prepare to jump, turn to page 113.

"Hold on. I'll get you aboard," you say.

Leaning over as far as possible, you grab the man by the collar of his coat and heave him upward. He splutters and splashes, flapping on the gunwale like a fish. The rifle is gone.

The man flops into the boat, soaked, exhausted, but perhaps still dangerous.

You move to the stern, grasping one of the oars as a weapon in case he launches an attack, and manage to start the outboard. Relying on instinct, you head toward the darkened outline of the island. The searchlights from the ferry crisscross the water. You hear the powerful roar of the launch across the waves.

Soon you turn into a cove on the shoreline. The cove is protected by a series of large rocks that are bathed in the swell of the waves. The launch is patrolling back and forth. Your boat comes to rest with a crunch on the pebbly, sandy beach.

"Don't say a thing," you whisper to your prisoner.

He nods to affirm the command.

Turn to page 106.

You've only taken a few steps when a voice stops you.

"Halt, who goes?" asks the firm voice.

"The light of the world," Wogan replies.

"Welcome," is the response.

A man dressed in the rough clothes of a herdsman leads you to two horses tethered to a low-lying tree. A map, a compass, and a wish for good luck are given to you. Then you are off. There is no time to rest; it is a long way to the border, and the people who want Wogan are relentless. The trip will hold many dangers.

"Who was that man?" you ask Wogan, wondering how extensive Wogan's network is.

"A cousin. I'm related to many in these parts," Wogan says.

Turn to page 79.

The stream of people getting off the ferry merges with those now getting on for the return trip to the mainland. It is quite easy to lose oneself in the crowd. Surveying the dock, you realize to your dismay that the man identified as a Yenrotta is no longer to be seen! Where is he? you wonder. Maybe he's aboard the ferry. You turn to warn the woman, but she's gone!

Turn to page 73.

"Get down. Don't provide them with a target."

"Who are they?" you ask.

"Crooks, thieves, spies. Who cares? They want you and Wogan. They have been following you from London just as we have."

You look at the man in surprise, but he just pulls the starter rope, and the outboard coughs and then sputters into a steady but not very powerful chugging. The boat heads into the wind and rides the waves.

There is water in the bottom of the boat, water mixed with oil and gas from years of use. You huddle down in the slime, hands resting on a thwart.

"Where are we going?" you ask.

"You'll see. Leave it to me," is the man's reply.

The launch is gaining. Off to the port side you see one more flare arch across the sky. It's a dud and falls harmlessly to the sea.

Turn to page 100.

The driver motions for you to get off the bus. You do, and then you are told to follow the men into the villa. Wogan's daughter goes with you. Dimmed flashlights are used to guide you through long hallways until you reach a medium-sized room.

"Wogan!" you say in a loud, surprised voice.

"Welcome, young friend. Time is of the essence. I must move fast," Wogan says.

"Why?" you ask. "Isn't the island safe?"

"No! We have just arrived and already they know where we are. The key to world peace is the radiation neutralizer. We must finish it and give the plans to the world. I went into hiding to try to finish it on my own, but I've had enemy agents on my trail since the beginning. I've got to leave Bozcaada. I've escaped from Canakkale, where I was held prisoner, and the agents are still after me."

"How will you go?" you ask.

"Boat to the mainland, in disguise by horse to the border, then train, and finally plane," Wogan replies.

"But where to?" you ask.

Go on to the next page.

"Back to England," he responds. "I'm almost finished with the plans."

"Wogan, I want to come with you! You might need me. I'm your best protector! You always said I had a sixth sense about things—especially danger."

"Yes, you could help me escape, but perhaps I should give you my latest work. Then, if I'm captured, you can finish the plans. I have faith in you. I leave it up to you, my friend. You can stay here and finish the plans, if necessary, or you can come with me."

If you want to go with Wogan,
turn to page 49.

If you stay behind with the latest plans for the
radiation neutralizer, turn to page 75.

You hear three blasts on the horn, the ramp goes up, the powerful engines reverse, and the ferry moves away from the dock. You try to make yourself as small as possible, huddling among the crowd of people occupying the table where you sit in the passenger cafeteria. The smell of licorice and of strong black coffee permeates the room.

The Yenrotta suddenly appears in the cafeteria. He surveys the crowd carefully, searching, evaluating, searching again.

Turn to page 11.

"Lead me to him," you say, trying to sound brave and confident. Your legs feel like Silly Putty, your stomach like a cement mixer, and your heart like a jackhammer. "Lead me to him."

Wogan is sitting in a chair in the next room. His face is composed. He looks younger and happier than at any other time you've seen him. His color is good.

"He looks fine to me," you say.

"Yes, but he has been this way for six weeks—without food or water. He will die if he doesn't come out of the trance."

"He's in hibernation," you respond.

"Evidently. But his pulse rate is almost nonexistent. There's a limit to how long even famous yogis who practice this strange art can go on. I'm afraid of brain death."

Turn to page 90.

Loneliness settles over you as you watch Wogan leave for the mainland in his small boat. The people standing around you are silent and saddened also. That's always the way it is with Wogan, you think. People love him and become dedicated to him. "Well, let's get to it," you announce. "It's time to prepare for the worst. Inside now."

You surprise even yourself at how quickly you take command of the situation. Leadership is natural to you, but at your age, it still is surprising that these people—the bus driver, Wogan's daughter, and the men at the villa—all respond to you without questioning your authority.

Inside the villa, you ask them to gather around a table to plan for defense against attack and for your escape.

Turn to page 87.

You climb inside and the cab pulls away from the curb—but not before two people wearing fishermen's clothing climb in, one in front, the other in back next to you. They smell of garlic and tobacco.

"Let's get going," says the man sitting next to you. "We've got our catch for the day. This one is a fine specimen, no?"

The taxi accelerates and night swallows you in the folded hills of Bozcaada. You have been kidnapped, and you will be held for ransom. The ransom is probably Wogan and his plans. Your chances are not good.

The End

Toward noon, you see a band of men on horses moving in your direction. You look to Wogan to see if these men could be more "relatives." By the look on Wogan's face you know he wasn't expecting to see anyone.

If you decide to run for it, turn to page 105.

If you want to hide, turn to page 111.

Curiosity has always been one of your strong points, or so you have thought. The book that was placed or dropped next to the burlap bag is too tempting to ignore. It must have been put there for a reason. You open it to the pages where the bookmark rests.

Reading quickly, you guess that it is a translation of an old folk tale. It tells of a powerful leader who overcomes evil for the good of the people. This leader is constantly being chased, attacked, and harassed by gangs and groups of the evil and corrupt. The story sounds surprisingly familiar. You wonder how the book got here and why just reading it gives you a sense of peace.

Turn to page 26.

You don't trust your companion one bit, so you're not going to let him out of your sight.

You head up a steep slope, stumbling on the rocks in the dark. As you make your way, he chatters incessantly.

"You really should've trusted me. I really am one of Wogan's assistants. He's told me all about the radiation neutralizer. It's fascinating, especially the unfinished parts."

His constant talking irritates you. It's difficult to formulate a plan with all this talk.

"So," continues the man, "Wogan told me that you knew the rest of the plans. He intended to tell *me* but we had not time."

You know that you were right not to trust this man, but now what are you going to do? You are no closer to finding or helping Wogan than you were when you left Canakkale on the ferry. There's only one thing you can do—separate from this man and start over again.

Turn to page 88.

Silently, a stone wall slides open on gleaming metal hinges, revealing a stainless steel spiral staircase. A greenish light comes from below, a cool current of air blows up the steps. You hesitate.

"Go ahead. Have no fear," says the dwarf. This time his voice is no more than a faint whisper.

It takes several minutes to descend the stairs. At last you reach the source of the green light. It comes from a cavelike room of solid rock. The light is generated by a bank of computer monitors. Three people huddle over the central screen. They straighten up at the sound of your approach.

Turn to page 89.

84

Days later, you and Doctor Wogan wake up in a wildflower field high in some mountains. You vaguely remember lengthy interviews with your captors. The interviews were like friendly conversations. No force, no persuasion, only talk. Then there was a murky period, and now you are awake, alive, and in this pasture. You turn to the brilliant doctor. "Wogan?" you say.

He looks at you, puzzled. Then he says slowly, "I feel as if I'm waking from a bad dream. There are enormous gaps in what I can remember. They've tampered with my memory. . . . And they've got the radiation neutralizer."

The End

You believe this intense woman. There is even a distinct resemblance to Wogan. "Will you help?" she asks again.

You nod.

"Good," she replies. "Follow me. Wogan awaits us. It is three hours by foot to his hiding place. He has just arrived after escaping from a band of thieves in Canakkale. He was able to break away from them when the thieves were distracted by *your* arrival and began to follow your movements. Here, put on these clothes. From a distance we will pass for farmers."

You head off to meet Wogan and once again to be his close aide and assistant. With luck, the radiation neutralizer will be finished, and the world will finally have a defense against nuclear weapons.

The End

"So, who are they, what can we do, who will do what?" you ask, looking at each face carefully.

Wogan's daughter answers. "They are a group of international criminals who deal in drugs, slavery, espionage, and anything else that will turn a profit. They operate like a business. They are efficient, brutal, and dedicated—dedicated to money. They want those plans."

"So what do we do?" you ask again.

"We could join them," the bus driver answers, laughing in a loud voice.

At that moment a high piercing whine invades the room.

"Attack!" yells one of the villa guards.

You all dive for the floor just as a rocket explodes against the side of the villa.

*If you think you should surrender,
turn to page 3.*

If you want to take action, turn to page 58.

88

The burden of the world weighs heavily upon your shoulders. You are the human race's last hope. Your only clue to Wogan's whereabouts is that he had an island retreat in the Aegean Sea off the coast of Turkey. The name of the island is Bozcaada. The closest city on the mainland is Canakkale.

Three days later you have reached Canakkale. A poster on the stone wall of a church in a square immediately catches your attention. There's a picture of a man on the poster.

"It's Wogan! It's him!" you shout. Slowly you translate the poster with the aid of a Turkish phrase book. It says:

SPECIAL APPEARANCE OF ZABILLH
THE GREAT MIND READER
MARCH 9, 10:30 P.M.
PLACE TO BE ANNOUNCED
SIGN UP NOW AT HOTEL CHRISTOS

It is now 4:30 P.M.

Is the poster a sign meant especially for your eyes? And is the sign from Wogan—or from those against Wogan?

Turn to page 95.

"Here is one who is brave enough to meet Zabillh. Will this one do?" the dwarf asks.

"Yes. Perfectly," replies the figure in the center with a knowing grin. "Prepare our visitor."

A murmuring sound, not quite music, fills the room.

"That's Wogan's sound," you say, startled. Many times when you were Wogan's assistant, he would close his eyes, sit upright with arms and legs crossed, and emit a sound just like the one you are hearing. It is a sound made during meditation—the sound *om* repeated over and over again. Is Wogan making the sound, or is it someone else?

"Will you come now?" you are asked.

If you decide to go with them (and investigate the sounds on the way), turn to page 12.

If you try to escape (because you think this may be a set-up), turn to page 29.

You approach Wogan, glad to see him but worried that you might be making a mistake by trying to save him. Obviously Wogan is frightened by these people and does not trust them. That explains the trance, you think.

Wogan slowly moves his head. A look of wonder and sadness fills his eyes.

As you lean over him, he slides to the floor. You check his pulse. There is none. Wogan is gone. He takes his plans with him, except for what you know. Wogan has left you the enormous responsibility of being the sole caretaker of the secret of the radiation neutralizer. You look for a way out. There is none.

The End

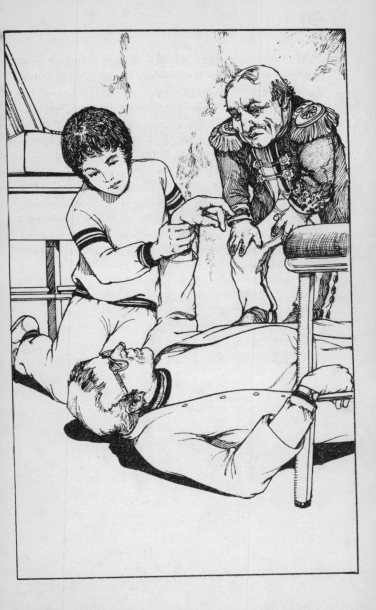

It is too dangerous to trust anyone yet. That woman could be an enemy, and she could easily push you into the water.

Maybe I'll be contacted on the island, you say to yourself.

The ferry sways in the waves, and you begin to experience a mixture of seasickness and fear.

The woman remains on the deck. She turns occasionally to stare at you, but she does not move, nor does anyone else in the cabin. It is unnaturally quiet. The only sound is the pumping beat of the ferry engine.

You realize you're going to be sick, and desperately look for a door to the deck that does not lead to the stern. You get to your feet, and, to your surprise, so does everyone else in the cabin. Then you notice that the ferry is at the dock. There is a thud as it gently bumps against the piers. With great relief you forget your seasickness and head for the landing ramp with the other passengers.

Turn to page 32.

"I've got to get out of here. I can't do much for Wogan until I get help."

You head for the spiral staircase and climb as quickly as you can. As you search frantically for the device that activates the stone wall, you wonder how long the effects of the action inhibitor last. Suddenly the wall slides open, and with great relief you enter the lobby of the hotel.

There, to your surprise, stands the brilliant Doctor Wogan. He's smiling.

"Well done, my young friend. Well done. Come with me. We have work to do. I knew I could count on you," he says.

"But I didn't do anything," you reply.

"Yes, you did. You inhibited their movement, thus releasing me from their power. They are strong, but we are stronger! Now, to complete our escape. Quickly! Let's be off! No time to waste. The world awaits our discovery."

The End

As you stare at the poster, a faint wind carrying the smell of rosemary and oregano sifts through the air. A middle-aged man slips on a cobblestone and bumps into you.

"Pardon me," he murmurs, while slipping a piece of paper into your hand. He moves off. The paper says: "Take the next ferry to the island of Bozcaada. You will be contacted. Beware of the lighted steps. Wogan lives, but there is great danger."

What now? you wonder. Should I trust this stranger?

If you decide to stay for the meeting with Zabillh, turn to page 6.

If you decide to go to Bozcaada by ferry, turn to page 4.

"I made it!" you yell in triumph as you reach the last step. Another shot rings out, but it bounces off the top step, not touching you.

You dash for the door, knocking over a fat man and his equally large wife who have just entered the hotel lobby.

"Sorry about that," you shout as you streak out into the square. You lose yourself in a crowd of people who are gathered around a series of open air stalls selling cheeses and meats, wine, sweaters, dried fruits, and old books.

You are safe now. Then, to your amazement, you turn and see Wogan standing next to you.

"Wogan! You're safe!" you exclaim.

"Thanks to you, I escaped in the confusion down there, but we must get to my island. Hurry. There isn't much time."

The End

The murmuring increases in intensity until it reverberates so much that you feel as though you were in a huge pinball machine, being bounced back and forth by the murmuring sound waves.

"I . . . MUS . . . T . . . WA . . . KE . . . U . . . P. . . ."

Immobilizing blackness slips into your shoes and floods upward through your body, until only your head is above it.

"Tell us what you know of Wogan!"

"What?" you manage to gasp.

"You know what!" the voice replies. "We have spies who tracked you from the moment you left Delta Group offices in London. We want information. Now tell us all you know."

If you pretend to pass out, turn to page 31.

If you decide to tell what you know, turn to page 34.

98

You push the force dial on the energy minimizer from +2 to +8.

A familiar voice fills the chamber.

"No! No! It's too much!" the voice yells.

It's Wogan!

"Okay, Wogan," you say. Frantically you reduce the effect of the energy minimizer by returning the dial to +2, and then beyond to −1.

Turn to page 110.

The launch accelerates and catches up with you.

"What now?" you demand.

"Nothing. Nothing for you," replies the man.

The launch is traveling alongside you, and you recognize the well-dressed man in the tweed overcoat. He signals with a wave of his hand and the engine of the rowboat is cut.

"This is as far as I go," says the pipe-smoker. "You're all theirs now. The people I work for aren't paying me enough for me to risk my own life. These folks can have you."

You are transferred roughly to the launch, which speeds off toward a rocky coastline at the southern end of the island. Soon you reach land.

In the dark you see a long stone staircase. Each step is lighted by a small bulb on the side of the step. At the top of the steps you dimly make out a group of buildings. No light shines in them.

"You will be staying here for quite some time," says the man in the tweed overcoat. "You have information we want, and we will get it." He retreats down the lighted steps, leaving you in the hands of two burly men.

The End

From the outer edge of the Milky Way galaxy a lone technician in an Orbital Heavens Observatory notes the sudden disappearance of a minor planet from the scanning screen.

The End

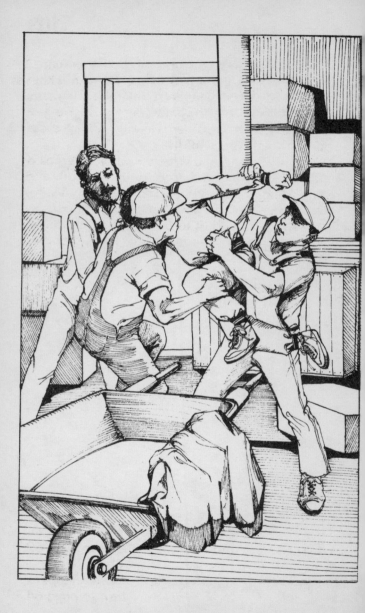

"I'm game, let's go," you say to the woman.

Once on the dock you follow her, but within minutes you are surrounded by a group of workers in blue coveralls. They grab you, thrust you in a large wheelbarrow, cover you with burlap sacks and hurriedly move off the dock.

You hear a shout, a woman's voice. Then all is quiet. You choke on the gag in your mouth and struggle against crude handcuffs of twisted wire. As soon as you free your hands you remove the gag. Just as you start to break out of the burlap bag, you are grabbed roughly and lifted, probably into a van or truck.

If you decide to put up a fight, turn to page 60.

*If you wait to see what happens,
turn to page 64.*

104

Dawn finds you safely hidden in an isolated farm shed on a hill above a small town. You can see the ferry at its dock. People are hurrying to get aboard for its morning run to the mainland. It seems so calm and tranquil from your vantage point on the hillside. The people and the boat are toylike. You feel as though you have awakened from a bad dream. Getting up, you stretch your arms to the sky. Suddenly, you feel a pistol barrel in the small of your back.

"Keep those hands up. Don't move or I'll be forced to shoot."

Turn to page 109.

"Wogan, get going, it's our only chance!" you yell, striking your horse with the crop and kicking hard. You don't get far. You are surrounded, captured, interrogated, and imprisoned, along with Wogan.

"My young friend, it seems like disaster, but wait, just wait," Wogan says to you as you sit together in the stone cell of your prison. "Patience. The plans they took from me are not only incomplete but deliberately misleading. Only you and I know how to interpret them properly. We'll never talk, will we?"

The End

106

The launch cruises by, penetrating the darkness with a powerful but narrow searchlight beam. There are so many rocks and inlets that you may remain undetected. Suddenly you realize the men must think you're still in the boat. You decide to start the motor, fix the steering, and push out to sea.

You do this, and the rowboat heads out, bumping across waves. You watch it gain the open water.

"Soon they'll pick it up. We don't have much time. Let's go," you say to your companion.

Turn to page 81.

"Help us with these papers. We must have the missing parts. Only then will Wogan be allowed to live, and you too." The man lights a cigarette and blows smoke rings slowly in your direction.

Wogan has warned you many times—has even made you swear—to protect the plans with your life. "In the right hands these plans mean *peace*. In the wrong hands they mean slavery on a scale beyond your wildest imagination." Those had been some of the last words spoken to you by Wogan before he disappeared.

You stall for time. The man presses you to make a decision. You pretend, talk, beg, ridicule. You are desperate, but you will not yield. His threats don't frighten you; the plans are useless without your vital information. Time is on your side, and both of you know it.

The End

Your captor signals to someone down the hill. Minutes later, to your amazement, the woman from the ferry arrives.

"I told you there was danger. I'm surprised you escaped. They meant to kill you," she says.

"It seems I'm no better off now," you answer, hands still stretched skyward.

"You can put your hands down now, but until I'm sure that you mean no harm to Wogan and his work, you will not be free."

It takes hours of talk to convince her that you are who you say you are.

You look around, noticing that the guard with the gun is relaxed and more interested in his cigar than in you.

"Who are you?" you ask.

"I'm Wogan's daughter," she replies.

"I never knew Wogan had a daughter," you say suspiciously.

"Even his close friends know little of the real Wogan. He was born on this island. You knew him only in your country. Enough talk. Yes or no? Will you help me or not? If you are who you say you are, he needs you to help finish the radiation neutralizer."

Turn to page 85.

There is a screeching, tearing sound as time and space collide for a fraction of a moment and then decay. The stone walls and ceiling and floor open up as the molecules lose their hold on one another. When one of the walls falls away, you see Wogan, a prisoner in the next room. You and Wogan make your escape; your captors seem overpowered by what has happened and make no move to stop you.

"What now, Wogan?" you ask.

"Back to London. We'll finish the radiation neutralizer there. It's probably safer, and I'm tired of trying to hide from all these thieves. Everyone wants our plans, but they want them just for themselves. We'll give the plans to the world. That's freedom."

The End

"Let's take cover, Wogan," you suggest breathlessly. "Maybe they haven't seen us. We can't outrun them." You are already off your horse.

"No! Try to escape," he urges you, and spurs his horse onward. He hands you a duplicate set of the unfinished plans. "Finish these if I'm caught. One of us must make it!" He gallops off.

You watch in horror as he is surrounded by other men who come from the opposite direction.

Now you are alone and in sole possession of the secrets.

"I must escape. I must succeed," you say as you scurry into the tangle of brush surrounding the rocky outcroppings of a small hill. "I must escape."

The End

You cast aside the volume. The leather bookmark falls out and the book slides to the far side of the van.

You hold onto the sides of the van for a moment, judging your chances for a successful leap. Then, putting care aside, you leap out, tucking into a ball and rolling when you hit the grassy bank by the side of the road.

Standing up, you watch the van bounce along into the distance.

"Well, I'm out of that one," you say with a sigh of relief. "Now to find Wogan."

The End

ABOUT THE AUTHOR

R.A. MONTGOMERY is an educator and publisher. A graduate of Williams College, he also studied in graduate programs at Yale University and New York University. After serving in a variety of administrative capacities at Williston Academy and Columbia University, he co-founded Waitsfield Summer School in 1965. Following that, Montgomery helped found a research and development firm specializing in the development of educational programs. He worked for several years as a consultant to the Peace Corps in Washington, D.C., and West Africa. He is now both a writer and a publisher.

ABOUT THE ILLUSTRATOR

LESLIE MORRILL is a designer and illustrator whose work has won him numerous awards. He has illustrated over thirty books for children, including the Bantam Classics edition of *The Wind in the Willows;* for the Bantam Skylark Choose Your Own Adventure series, *Indian Trail, Mona Is Missing, Attack of the Monster Plants,* and *Sand Castle;* and for the Choose Your Own Adventure series, *Lost on the Amazon, Mountain Survival, Danger at Anchor Mine,* and *Journey to the Year 3000,* a Bantam Super Adventure. His work has also appeared frequently in *Cricket* magazine. A graduate of the Boston Museum School of Fine Arts, Mr. Morrill lives near Boston, Massachusetts.

CHOOSE YOUR OWN ADVENTURE

VARSITY COACH

The all-new, action-packed Sports Series that will keep you cheering, page after page!

- ☐ 26033 FOURTH & GOAL #1
  Tommy Hallowell $2.50
- ☐ 26209 TAKEDOWN #2
  Leigh Franklin $2.50
- ☐ 26330 OUT OF BOUNDS #3
  Tommy Hallowell $2.50
- ☐ 26526 DOUBLE PLAY #4
  Lance Franklin $2.50

Look for them at your local bookstore, or use this handy coupon for ordering:

Special Offer
Buy a Bantam Book
for only 50¢.

Now you can order the exciting books you've been
wanting to read straight from Bantam's latest
listing of hundreds of titles. *And* this special offer
gives you the opportunity to purchase a Bantam
book for only 50¢. Here's how:

By ordering any five books at the regular price
per order, you can also choose any other single
book listed (up to $4.95 value) for only 50¢. Some
restrictions do apply, so for further details send
for Bantam's listing of titles today.

Just send us your name and address and we'll send
you Bantam Book's SHOP AT HOME CATALOG!